FRANCINE PASCAL'S

SWEET VALLEY High®

SLAM BOOK

by Laurie Pascal Wenk

BANTAM BOOKS
TORONTO · NEW YORK · LONDON · SYDNEY · AUCKLAND

For my grandmother, Kate Rubin

SWEET VALLEY HIGH SLAM BOOK
A Bantam Book/October 1988

Sweet Valley High is a registered trademark of Francine Pascal.
Conceived by Francine Pascal.
Produced by Daniel Weiss Associates, Inc.
27 West 20th Street,
New York, NY 10011
Cover by James Mathewuse.

ISBN 0-553-05496-1

Published simultaneously in the United States and Canada

Bantam Books are published by Bantam Books, a division of
Bantam Doubleday Dell Publishing Group, Inc. Its trademark,
consisting of the words "Bantam Books" and the portrayal of a
rooster, is Registered in U.S. Patent and Trademark Office and
in other countries. Marca Registrada. Bantam Books, 666 Fifth
Avenue, New York, New York 10103

PRINTED IN THE UNITED STATES OF AMERICA

S 0 9 8 7 6 5 4 3 2 1

Hi, everybody,

Something absolutely fabulous has just hit Sweet Valley High. It's called a slam book, and Jessica and I want to be the first ones to tell you about it. We have a feeling you're going to love it. We do.

A slam book is sort of a cross between a yearbook and an autograph book. You know the section in a yearbook where the best athlete or the smartest person is named? Well, in our book *you're* the one who gets to make those choices. And not only that, there are tons of categories on every subject imaginable.

Each Sweet Valley High *Slam Book* has two sections. The first one is the biggest and most important. That's for the best of everything, and it's separated into girls and boys. The second section is called the "Crystal Ball." That's where you get to guess what's going to happen to your classmates in the future.

Now that you can see how the book is set up, we'll tell you how to use it.

On the top of each page there is a heading such as "Most Talented" or "Most Popular." The rest of the page is blank. Your job is to write in the name of the person you think best fits the category. For example, under "Most Loyal Friend" I would write Enid Rollins. Or under "Class Clown" I would definitely write Winston Egbert. (In fact, in some categories Jessica and I have already written in our choices.) After you finish each category, you fold the page on the dotted line to keep your choice private.

You go through the whole book, entering all the names you want. Then you and your friends trade, and you write your choices in one another's books. Be sure to put your own name on the inside cover so your book doesn't get confused with those of your friends.

Another very important point—this book should be passed around *only* during free periods or at lunchtime. It's too distracting during classes, so we've decided to make it a rule not to use it during class time. The most important thing to remember about the slam book is that it's supposed to be fun. We don't want to hurt anyone's feelings. That's no fun at all. I even got Jessica to agree to that.

But she wants me to tell you that *she's* added a little spice to make it more exciting. She wanted to fill the book with categories such as "Best Looking," "Biggest Flirt," and "Best Gossip"—and that's where we disagreed.

I'm more interested in choosing things like "Best Athlete" or "Smartest." Jessica says that's goody-goody stuff and *boring*. Can't you just hear her saying that? Well, we couldn't agree, so we decided to take turns making up categories.

One last reminder—make sure to use a pen so no one can change anything. Have fun!

Sincerely,

Elizabeth Wakefield

P.S. Don't forget, you can write in your own name if you happen to think you really are the best looking, the most popular and have the greatest clothes.

Love Ya,

Jessica

P.P.S. Or you just happen to be the most conceited!

E.

P.P.P.S. As you use the slam book, you'll notice a special treat. Liz and I have written down, in letter form, some of the advice our friends have asked us for. Plus, we've added an extra special horoscope and a calendar at the end of the book. Enjoy!

J.

GIRLS

Most Like Elizabeth Wakefield

Dear Jessica,

    I've been going out with this guy for five months now, but I think he's interested in someone else, although he hasn't said anything about it to me. I really like him. Do you think I should dump him before he dumps me?

Confused

Dear Confused,

    Since you like him and since he hasn't mentioned anything about another girl, you should be sure before you do anything drastic. Don't be so quick to give up.

J.

Most Like Jessica Wakefield

Dear Elizabeth,

My mom and I get along pretty well except in one major area. She won't let me date. I'm thirteen years old, and she thinks I'm too young. What should I do?

Possible Old Maid

Dear Old Maid,

Why don't you calmly talk to your mother about going out with a group of kids, instead of on a date with one person? If you start off slowly and show her that you can be trusted, I'm sure she'll feel more at ease.

E.

Most Popular

Elizabeth Wakefield

Jessica Wakefield

Dear Jessica,

My best friend and I always double date. Lately every time I ask her if she wants to, she acts funny. I can't figure it out, and I'm worried about losing her friendship.

Worried

Dear Worried,

Obviously there's something wrong. Do you think it's possible she has a crush on your boyfriend? The best thing for you to do is ask her why she doesn't want to double date anymore. If she is really your best friend, you'll be able to work it out.

J.

Biggest Flirt

Dear Elizabeth,

I'm thirteen and worried about my reputation. I used to be friends with a bunch of girls. We had a fight and we're not friends anymore. I've been hearing some very untrue rumors going around, and I don't know what to do.

Worried

Dear Worried,

Isn't it terrible when people say mean things just to get back at you? The best you can do is ignore them, even though it's hard. The rumors will die down in time. It has happened to all of us.

E.

Best Athlete

Dear Jessica,

I'm going away for two months during the summer to be a junior counselor. I'm fifteen and have been dating this guy for eight months. He's worried I'll meet someone at camp. I love him, and I don't want him to be upset.

In Love

Dear In Love,

Personally, I don't believe in getting tied down to one person. This might be a good opportunity for you to meet someone new. If you're truly set on this guy, though, and don't intend to date all summer long, then all you can do is try to make him feel secure. One way of doing that is by writing him a lot from camp. Let him know you care. It's worked for my sister Liz!

J.

Most Talented

Dana Larson

Dear Elizabeth,

I've been writing the gossip column for the school newspaper for two years. I'm getting a little tired of it, and I feel ready to write some news stories. Nobody will take me seriously. I need some advice.

                                                                    Writer

Dear Writer,

The only way you're going to get people to take you seriously is to write a good, solid news story and show it to your editor. The newspaper staff is probably just so used to your doing the gossip column, they can't imagine your doing anything else. Believe me, I know what it's like. I had the same problem once, but it all worked out fine. Now I write news stories *and* the "Eyes and Ears" column. Good luck!

                                                                    E.

Smartest

Dear Jessica,

I'm fourteen and have a curfew of ten o'clock. All my friends stay out till eleven or midnight on weekends. How can I get my parents to understand that I'm old enough to take care of myself?

Responsible

Dear Responsible,

Ten o'clock does seem a little unreasonable to me. Have you asked your parents what their concerns are? Try that, and then let them know that you don't mind coming home at ten, but when there are parties or special occasions you'd like to be able to come home later. If they agree to let you stay out later, be sure you're home on time. I have trouble doing that myself and believe me, it's important!

J.

Best Dancer

Dear Elizabeth,

I'm thirteen and my mother won't let me wear makeup. She says I'm too young. All my friends are wearing it, and I feel out of place. It's so unfair.

Unfair

Dear Unfair,

Tell your mother you've come up with a compromise. What if you started off with a little mascara and light lip gloss? Don't use anything else for a while. Let her get used to the idea gradually.

E.

Cutest

Dear Jessica,

 I'm thirteen and my boyfriend is fourteen. I feel like all he ever wants to do is kiss and make out. Sometimes I think he likes me just for that.

All Puckered Out

Dear Puckered Out,

 Maybe he does. Try not kissing him so much and see what happens!

J.

Best Kisser

Dear Elizabeth,

My best friend has been telling another friend some
things I told her in confidence. I feel like she has betrayed
me, and I'm very upset. How should I handle this situation?

Disappointed

Dear Disappointed,

Before you say anything, you have to be absolutely sure
that your best friend betrayed you. If she did, go to her and
let her know how you feel. Be honest and tell her you're not
sure you'll ever be able to trust her again.

E.

Best Gossip

Caroline Pearce

Dear Jessica,

For the past several months, I have been baby-sitting for a neighbor on a steady basis. I usually take along a friend. Suddenly I've been baby-sitting for this neighbor less and less and she's been baby-sitting for her more. I'm mad!

Mad

Dear Mad,

I can understand why you're angry—I'd be furious! Why don't you try asking your friend about it? She must have an idea why this is happening. Explain to her that this is your job and it's wrong for her to baby-sit when you are available. Tell her you will gladly help her find her own jobs.

J.

Most Conceited

Dear Elizabeth,

I'm thirteen and have two brothers. One is eleven and the other is nine and a half. It seems that whenever anything goes wrong, I get blamed. Why do my brothers always get away with everything?

Help Me

Dear Help Me,

Sometimes parents think that the oldest child should set the example for the younger ones. Then maybe the others won't make the same mistakes. This could be why it seems that your parents blame everything on you. It couldn't hurt to explain to them how you feel the next time it happens.

E.

Best Dressed

Lila Fowler

Dear Jessica,

   I'm fifteen and I like this guy who is fourteen. My friends
tease me about him. Is it that awful to go out with a guy
who's younger than I am?

                                                    Older Woman

Dear Older,

   Even though I usually prefer older men, I once got
involved with someone younger. If you truly like each other
and you both feel comfortable in the relationship, it's fine.
Don't worry so much about what other people think.

                                          J.

Most Loyal Friend

Enid Rollins

Cara Walker

BOYS

Most Like Bruce Patman

Dear Jessica,

    I'm a freshman and crazy about this guy who's a sophomore at my school. He doesn't even know I exist. How can I get him to notice me?

                             Invisible

Dear Invisible,

    It's not going to be easy since you're in different classes. Maybe you can try to talk to him during lunch. If that doesn't work, find out his schedule and try bumping into him on purpose. Then let it go from there. Good luck!

                             J.

Most Popular

Dear Elizabeth,

What do you do when your best friend wants to cheat from your test paper? We study together, but she's so worried about failing that just to make sure she doesn't, she wants to see my paper.

Scared to Cheat

Dear Scared,

You must tell your friend that cheating is not something either of you should be doing. It's not fair for you to jeopardize your grades just so she can be sure she is giving the right answers. If you get caught, you'll both be in big trouble! If she's your friend, she'll understand.

E.

Biggest Flirt

Dear Jessica,

I have a friend who always makes these great plans with me, but at the last minute she finds some reason to cancel, and I end up staying at home. She's becoming more of a disappointment all the time. I want to say something to her, but I don't want to lose her friendship. I still like her.

Stay-at-Home

Dear Stay,

You may like this friend, but she doesn't seem to be very considerate. Try this: Don't make any plans with her for a while and see what happens. If she doesn't get the message, tell her that you're hurt and why. If she cancels again— find another friend to do things with!

J.

Biggest Jock

Ken Matthews

Dear Jessica,

I'm fourteen and have been dating this guy for a few months now. The problem is that he likes spending time with the guys—and that doesn't include me. I'm getting a little suspicious. Do you think I should be?

Stuck Home

Dear Stuck,

It depends on how many times a week he likes to be with the guys. Is he really overdoing it? Talk to him if you think so, but don't make him feel as if you don't trust him.

J.

Smartest

Peter DeHaven

Dear Elizabeth,

My mother is always complaining about what a mess my room is. I tell her it's my room and I like it that way. She says it's her house and if I don't keep it clean she's going to start taking some of my privileges away. Am I wrong?

Sloppy but Happy

Dear Sloppy,

I'm not sure if this is a right or wrong situation, but sometimes you have to give in because it's not worth the arguments.

E.

Best Dancer

Dear Jessica,

I'm thirteen and fed up. My parents won't let me make or get phone calls during the week. They say it interferes with my homework. Everybody else I know is allowed to talk on the phone. It's embarrassing.

Unhappy

Dear Unhappy,

I'm not surprised that you feel this way. If my parents didn't let me talk on the phone, I think I'd die! Why don't you try to work out an arrangement so that you can use the phone for a half hour every night? Hope it works!

J.

Best Kisser

Dear Elizabeth,

I'm fourteen and I just moved to a new town. I miss my old friends so much. I'm miserable.

Miserable

Dear Miserable,

It's hard to make new friends, but you'll be happier if you try. It doesn't mean you have to forget the old ones. Maybe during your next vacation you can go visit them. That will give you something to look forward to!

E.

Best Looking

Dear Jessica,

    I've been hanging around with what my mother's heard is a bad crowd. We all go to the same high school, and believe me, there's nothing wrong with these kids. How can I convince my mother of that?

                                        Upset

Dear Upset,

    The best way to show your mother what your friends are like is to have her meet them. Invite them over for dinner so she can see for herself.

                                          J.

Most Talented

Guy Chesney

Dear Elizabeth,

I've been tricked! I've wanted my ears pierced for so long. When I was ten my mother said I could have it done when I became a teenager. Well, I just turned thirteen, and now she says I have to wait till I'm sixteen. What can I say to her so that she'll change her mind?

Tricked

Dear Tricked,

Tell her that it wasn't fair for her to say okay and then take it back. Tell her you've been looking forward to this for three years and you are very disappointed. You trusted her and you feel as though she's deceived you.

E.

Class Clown

Winston Egbert

Dear Jessica,

I'm fourteen and most of my friends smoke. I've tried it a few times and I really don't like it, but my friends keep pressuring me. What should I do?

Non-Smoker

Dear N.S.,

Smoking is dangerous and a terrible habit. And your hair and clothes will smell bad, too. Yuck! Tell your friends to stop pressuring you and encourage them to quit. It's not cool!

J.

Nicest

Tom McKay

CRYSTAL BALL

Couple of the Future

Dear Jessica,

There's this friend of mine who is always hanging around. She never knows when to go home, and worst of all, she always manages to be there when I'm with my boyfriend. I'm no dummy. I know she likes him. She even flirts with him right in front of me. I want to say something to her, but I'm afraid I'll hurt her feelings.

Afraid to Hurt

Dear Afraid,

Well, she's not afraid to hurt **your** feelings, and to tell the truth, she doesn't sound like much of a friend to me! Tell her straight out that if she wants to be your friend, she'd better leave your boyfriend alone.

J.

Most Likely to Marry First

Dear Elizabeth,

I'm fourteen, and I've been spending Saturdays with my grandmother since I was a little girl. I love her, but weekends are when all my friends get together. I want to spend time with my grandmother, but not every Saturday. I'm afraid to tell her because I don't want to hurt her feelings.

Grandma's Girl

Dear Grandma's Girl,

Your grandmother knows you love her. That's obvious. Next Saturday when you see her, tell her just what you told me. Maybe you can arrange to see her for dinner during the week instead. Most grandmothers are happy to see their grandchildren at any time!

E.

Most Likely to Be A Movie Star

Dear Jessica,

    I'm an identical twin, too. I just met a new guy at school, and he seemed to like me. Then he met my sister, and ever since he hasn't said a word to me. I'm so mad and hurt. What should I do?

                                        Hurt

Dear Hurt,

    I have to admit this is a tough one for me to answer because on occasion I have liked the same boy as Elizabeth. Maybe you could pretend to be your twin until the guy recognizes you as the more beautiful, charming, sophisticated one. No! I'm kidding. Don't do that. Tell your sister you're interested in this guy and then try to make an arrangement with her: Neither one of you will go after the other's potential boyfriends.

                                      J.

Most Likely to Be A Millionaire

Dear Elizabeth,

   I've been dating this guy who's eighteen and I'm fifteen. I don't think it's a big deal, but I know my parents wouldn't approve, so I've been keeping it a secret. Then my brother found out. Now he keeps teasing me and saying he'll tell my parents. I'm a wreck.

                                    Nervous

Dear Nervous,

   It's not going to be easy, but why don't you gently tell your parents? If they're going to be mad, they'll be less mad hearing it from you instead of your brother. Unless there's something wrong with this guy, I don't see why they won't approve.

                                    E.

Most Likely to Have Six Kids

Dear Jessica,

A few of the kids in my class smoke pot and one of them is my sister's boyfriend. Drugs are so dangerous, and I'm sure if my sister knew she would be very upset. I'm worried that she will want to try it, too. I'm caught in the middle. What should I do?

Concerned

Dear Concerned,

As you say, drugs are dangerous. Sometimes you have to betray a confidence to protect someone you love. Tell your sister what you know about her boyfriend. At least she'll be aware of the problem, and she can make her own decision about what to do. People think I'm more daring than Elizabeth, but when it comes to drugs, we think exactly alike. They're killers!

J.

Most Likely to Be President

Dear Jessica,

I don't think my English teacher likes me, probably because it always seems I'm unprepared when she calls on me. The truth is it makes me really nervous to speak in front of the class. Should I say something to her?

Tongue Tied

Dear Tongue Tied,

Of course you should! Tell her that it's always been hard for you to speak in front of a group but you are making an effort to improve this problem. Try to get the teacher on your side. Once she understands your problem, I have a feeling she'll be easier on you, and after a while, it might be even easier for you to speak up.

J.

HOROSCOPE

ARIES (March 21–April 20)

You are a natural-born leader, but you sometimes come on a bit too strong. Try not to worry so much about what others think of you. You are a good and loyal friend, and lots of people seek you out for those qualities. You love to start new projects but have trouble sticking with them until the end. This is because patience is not one of your strong points. Boys are naturally drawn to your warmth and your sense of adventure.

TAURUS (April 21–May 21)

You can be as stubborn as the bull your sign is named for and you don't like being told what to do. However, expressing yourself is something you do beautifully and with your Taurus creativity, you're a natural actress and singer. Boys are attracted to your strength and imagination, and they are impressed that you are so able to take care of yourself. Be careful that your cool, calm attitude doesn't give the guy you like the impression you're not interested.

GEMINI (May 22–June 21)

You've got a great sense of humor, and you love to laugh. That's why you're so popular. Your uncontrollable enthusiasm leads you to get involved in several projects at once. Be careful not to let any one of them overwhelm you. You tend to talk a lot (Does the teacher seem to catch you talking in class more than anyone else?) and are very straightforward. You are often late, for school and for dates. If you pay more attention to time, the rewards will be great.

CANCER (June 22–July 23)

Watch out for those mood swings! Your ultrasensitivity could cost you a friend; learn to forgive innocent mistakes. You are always looking for a new challenge. Your intuitive nature sometimes seems to scare those around you because they think you can read their minds. But boys find this fascinating, and they are drawn to your sensitivity and that knack you have for always being in the right place at the right time.

LEO (July 24–August 23)

you may break one too many hearts along the way. In spite of your reputation for always wanting to be the center of attention, you are modest and you spend as much time praising others as you do praising yourself. You are proud, dynamic, and generous. Your impulsiveness leads you to make rash decisions sometimes. Be careful. Think things through.

VIRGO (August 24–September 23)

Friends rely on you for your good judgment, especially your talent for organizing. You are a neatness freak and are easily upset when things are out of order. Not content with the way things are, you like to shake things up and introduce your fellow classmates to new experiences and activities. In spite of this, you are sometimes too quiet and could benefit from opening up a little more.

LIBRA (September 24–October 23)

You're not always as dependable as you could be, but you're so much fun to be with, your friends tend to overlook that quality. You are often called upon to settle disputes among your peers because you are patient, gentle, and fair-minded. Your playful nature sometimes gets you into trouble, but underneath it all, your tender, caring disposition shines through.

SCORPIO (October 24–November 22)

You can be a powerful leader when it comes to initiating new ideas. Friends are important to you, and loyalty is a must. But you love to compete with your friends, and your envious nature sometimes gets in the way of your friendships. You don't like it when others keep secrets from you, but you love knowing and keeping secrets. You are an incurable romantic, and boys seem to know that when you fall in love, it's for keeps.

SAGITTARIUS (November 23–December 21)

You tend to be overly critical and judgmental, and you could be hurting someone's feelings—maybe even those of a boy you care for. You are known for being level-headed, and when others come to you with their romantic problems, you don't hesitate to drop everything and help solve them. For you, however, self-reliance is the rule. You'd rather make do without the help of others. When you fall in love, you tend to fall hard.

CAPRICORN (December 22–January 20)

You love to learn, so school is fun for you, especially because you work well under pressure and always meet your deadlines. You're also persuasive, and you'll have no problem landing a good after-school job to make extra money. But have you noticed your tendency to become a little too materialistic? Watch out! It could become a problem, especially if you're too busy counting pennies to notice the really important things happening around you.

AQUARIUS (January 21–February 19)

Although someone once took advantage of your warm and giving nature, you shouldn't change. Just be more careful about your choice of friends in the future. You are a free spirit and like spending time alone. You also enjoy breaking rules and acting unpredictably. Don't let this get you into trouble in school. Boys adore your terrific sense of humor and are attracted to your intensity.

PISCES (February 20–March 20)

Those who don't know you well may call you meek and mild. But behind that quiet exterior lies a mysterious, glamorous soul. The enjoyment you find in creating illusions about yourself extends to the kind of work you like to do, too: you can be found holding the power behind the scenes, where the real action is. It also makes you good at detecting deceptions: if you suspect someone is lying to you, you're probably right.

JANUARY

FEBRUARY

MARCH

APRIL

MAY

JUNE

JULY

AUGUST

SEPTEMBER

OCTOBER

NOVEMBER

DECEMBER